STALKED BY THE NAVY SEAL

EMMA BRAY

CHAPTER
ONE

Tanner

THE WHEELS of the bus groan to a stop, and I'm stepping onto the sun-baked pavement of my old stomping grounds. Damn, it's been ages. My boots kick up a small cloud of dust on the familiar sidewalk leading into town, every step stirring the butterflies in my gut. Excitement pulses through me like a live wire —I'm back, baby.

"God, I've missed this place," I mutter to myself, squinting against the glare of the midday sun. The scent of fresh-cut grass and home-cooked meals wafting from open windows is a stark contrast to the sterile sea air I've been marinating in for far too long.

I don't even bother with a detour. Straight to Jake's place—it's like my feet know the way by heart. They carry me past Main Street, where laughter and local gossip weave through the air like music. But I'm all about that bass line of anticipation humming in my veins. This reunion's gonna be epic.

Jake's house comes into view, looking just like I remember—porch swing swaying lazily, the screen door a little crooked. I bound up the steps two at a time, adrenaline replacing the travel fatigue that's been clinging to my shoulders.

"Surprise, motherfucker!" I shout as I hammer my fist against the door, the sound echoing in the quiet neighborhood. A dog barks somewhere in the distance, but all I can focus on is the thumping of my own heart. Feels like it's ready to bust out of my chest and do a jig right there on the porch.

When the door swings open, I'm hit with the sight of Jake's shit-eating grin, and man, does it feel good to be home.

"Bro!" Jake's voice is a booming welcome as he lunges forward, his arms wrapping around me like I'm the last life preserver in a shipwreck. He's all warmth and muscle and that familiar scent of sawdust and aftershave. "You're finally back, man. Damn, I've missed you."

"Missed you too, Jake," I chuckle, patting his back

with a solid thud. We break apart and I can't help but feel this sense of rightness slotting into place. Home isn't just a place—it's this, the bear hugs and unspoken bonds.

"Look at you, all Navy SEAL'd out." He punches my shoulder playfully, sizing me up with a proud smirk. "You've got stories for days, I bet."

"More than you can handle," I shoot back, the banter as easy as breathing.

And then *she* walks in—Molly. Holy hell.

"Hey, Tanner," she says, her voice smooth as honey, and something inside me shifts uncomfortably. It's like someone cranked the thermostat way up. Her smile is a thousand watts bright, and it's doing funny things to my insides. Funny, dangerous things.

"Hey, Molly." My reply comes out half-strangled because damn, when did little Molly become a vision of jeans hugging curves in all the right places? Her brown hair cascades over her shoulders like a dark waterfall, and those eyes—like warm chocolate—are full of life, dancing with something that looks a lot like mischief.

"Welcome home," she adds, and the simple words feel like an invitation to something I'm pretty sure I should decline. But hell if I don't want to RSVP 'yes' on the spot.

"Thanks," I manage, hoping my voice doesn't betray

the sudden kickstart of my pulse. Because this is Jake's sister. Off-limits territory. And yet, here I am, already crossing lines in my head.

"Damn, you've grown up," I blurt out before I can stop myself. The words hang awkwardly between us, but it's the truth—Molly stands there, not at all the gawky teenager I waved goodbye to years ago.

Jake laughs, clapping a hand on my shoulder, breaking the tension. "Tanner, meet my sister again. Molly, this is Tanner. But you remember him, right?"

"Of course," she replies with a laugh that tinkles in the air, and we shake hands. Her grip is firm, confident, and I swear I feel a jolt zing up my arm. It's like touching a live wire—a really pretty live wire.

"Nice to see you again, Tanner," she says, looking up at me through those lashes. Jesus, her eyes should come with a warning label.

"Likewise," I say, and it's an understatement. My heart's doing double time in my chest, and I'm trying real hard not to let my gaze wander down the curve of her neck. *Keep it together, man.*

"Been a while since Jake had any friends over," Molly teases, and I catch a spark of fun in her eyes. She's enjoying this, the back-and-forth, and I can't help but join in.

"Maybe he's been scaring them off," I suggest, aiming for light, playful. Inside, my stomach does a slow roll because, damn, the way she smiles should be illegal.

"Or maybe they just couldn't handle my raw charisma," Jake counters, and we all chuckle, the sound rich and easy.

"Raw something," Molly mumbles under her breath, and I stifle a laugh. This girl, she's got wit sharp as a tack.

"Careful, sis," Jake warns, but his tone is fond, "Remember who's side you're on."

"Always yours," she shoots back, but her eyes linger on me, and I feel like we're sharing some kind of secret joke.

My brain tells me to step back, but every other damn part of me wants to lean in. To what? I have no clue. But the pull is there, magnetic and undeniable. And if I'm being honest with myself, which I try to avoid whenever possible, it's freaking intoxicating.

"Well, don't just stand there. Come on in." Jake motions me to his living room.

I flop down onto the beat-up couch, the familiar scent of his place flooding my senses—part detergent, part something fried. It's like I never left. The room is a time capsule of our high school shenanigans; posters of rock bands and a dartboard with a suspiciously Jake-shaped silhouette drawn on it.

"Man, remember when we tried to set up that backyard wrestling ring?" Jake laughs, cracking open a beer and handing one to me.

"Remember? I still have the scar." I roll up my sleeve to show off a faded line near my elbow. "Courtesy of your 'elbow drop of doom'."

He snorts, taking a swig. "You loved it. Admit it, Tanner. You were the best villain 'The Crusher' could've asked for."

"Villain? Dude, I was the misunderstood antihero," I protest, but I'm grinning so wide my cheeks hurt. We're lost in the past for a second, just two guys reliving their glory days.

"Antihero, my ass. You cheated every chance you got," he accuses, but there's zero heat in it.

"Strategy, bro. All about strategy." I wink at him, and we both crack up.

"Strategy," Molly echoes, stepping into the living room. Her head tilts, curiosity lighting up those big brown eyes. "What kind of strategies does a Navy SEAL have for backyard wrestling?"

"Ah, can't reveal all my secrets," I say, the words tumbling out easier than I expect. "But let's just say they involve a lot of stealth and not getting caught."

"Sounds scandalous," she teases, tucking a strand of hair behind her ear, and damn if I don't want to be that strand of hair.

"Only the best kind of scandalous," I shoot back. My heart's doing this stupid acrobatic thing because she's looking at me with interest that feels a shade too warm to be just friendly.

"Tell me more about being a SEAL," Molly says, settling down across from us. She's all eagerness and anticipation, like a kid before Christmas, and it knocks the wind right outta me.

"Which part?" I ask, voice rougher than I intend. "The adrenaline, the danger, or the endless push-ups?"

"Start with the adrenaline," she decides, and I dive into a story, leaving out the classified bits and the darkest parts. Instead, I paint her a picture of skydiving into unknown territory, the rush of ocean waves during a midnight swim, and the bond between brothers-in-arms.

She listens, rapt, her lips parted slightly. Every now and then, she throws in a question, and each one shows she's really listening, not just hearing. It's like she's peeling back layers I didn't even know I was wearing.

"Sounds like quite the adventure," she murmurs when I finish.

"Best and hardest years of my life," I admit, feeling exposed under her gaze. But her smile is soft, encouraging, and I find myself wanting to tell her more, to share parts of me I usually keep locked down tight.

"Must be nice to be home, though," she says. And yeah, it is. More than nice. It's necessary, like a deep breath after surfacing from deep underwater.

"Home has its perks," I agree, and for a heartbeat, I let my gaze linger on her, feeling that magnetic pull stronger than ever.

She bites her lower lip, and I feel my cock surge to full mast in my pants. I cough and shift on the couch, praying to God that Tanner won't see the huge tent I'm pitching for his sister right here in his living room.

Jesus, he'd beat me senseless, and I'd deserve it.

"Why don't I go grab us a few more?" I ask Jake, desperate for a moment of reprieve so I can readjust myself.

"You're our guest, man. I can get them."

"No," I insist as I hurriedly jump up. "Let me." I practically sprint into the kitchen like my ass is on fire.

Fuuuck.

I lean against the kitchen counter, popping a cap off another beer as laughter spills from the living room. Jake's got an arsenal of jokes, but it's Molly's laughter that's got me hooked, light and genuine, threading through the air like music.

"Want one?" I offer her as she wanders in, the fridge light casting a glow on her face.

"Sure," she replies, and her fingers brush mine as I

hand her a soda. An electric jolt shoots up my arm, and I'm pretty sure it's not static.

"What? No beer for me?" She raises a delicate eyebrow, and I eye her.

"No way, sweetheart. I know you're not old enough, and Jake would beat my ass if I gave you one."

She pouts prettily. "I'm nineteen. Technically old enough to die for my country like you, so I think I should be old enough to drink alcohol."

I size her up, and then her shoulders slump as she finally confesses, "Actually, I hate the taste of beer anyway."

I chuckle at that, and then I go quiet as I wonder who gave her a beer before. Was it another guy? Did he kiss her? Touch her? My grip tightens aroudn my beer as I try to tamp down the sudden jealousy that pumps through me at the thought of another man's hands on her.

Instead, I discreetly study her. Her cherubic face with puffy pink lips. The slight blush to her cheeks. The way her long brown hair sways with each move-ment she makes.

We settle into a comfortable silence, leaning side by side against the cool granite. She sips her drink, and I can't help but notice the way her throat moves, the soft curve of her lips. Damn, this is not the little girl I left behind.

"Your stories are insane," she says after a beat, her eyes wide with wonder. "You've really lived."

"Something like that," I say with a chuckle, the memory of danger and adrenaline still a shadow in my mind. But it's different now, sharing it with her. It feels almost cleansing.

"Would you do it all over again?" she asks, tilting her head, the brown locks tumbling over her shoulder.

"Every damn day," I answer without hesitation. But as I look at her, something inside me shifts, suggesting that maybe there's more to life than what I've known.

The hours slip by unnoticed, dusk turning to evening, the room bathed in the warm glow of sunset. We're nestled on the couch now, Jake monopolizing the conversation with tales of local drama, but Molly and I, we're in our own little world.

Our knees touch, just barely, but it's like a fire's lit between us. I sneak a glance at her, and find her already looking my way, a knowing smile dancing on her lips. I return it, my heart thudding a wild rhythm.

As the night deepens, shadows play across Molly's face, giving her this ethereal beauty that's hard to ignore. My eyes keep darting to her, like she's a magnet and I'm just a pile of iron shavings. There's an unspoken conversation happening in those stolen glances, questions and answers we're both too hesitant to voice out loud.

"More stories, Tanner?" Molly's voice is softer now, almost intimate. And hell, if I could, I'd spin tales until the sun comes up just to keep her looking at me that way. But I hold back because there's something terrifying about this, about how much I want to spill my guts to her.

"Maybe another time," I say, the words thick in my throat. "Don't wanna bore you with war stories all night."

"Impossible," she whispers, and the promise in her eyes is something fierce.

We share another secret smile, and yeah, I'm screwed. Because every look, every innocent touch, is cracking open the door to something I'm not sure I'm ready for. But right now, I let myself bask in the warmth of her presence, the night young and full of possibilities.

I inch closer to the edge of the couch, my body tensed as if I'm preparing for an unseen enemy. The tangle in my gut tightens with each laugh that Molly's voice sends echoing through the room. She's sitting there, cross-legged on the armchair, her eyes lighting up with every anecdote Jake and I toss into the air, and it's like watching a live wire spark—dangerous but impossible to look away from.

"Damn, you've really turned this place around, Jake," I comment, throwing a glance around the room, trying to distract myself from the girl who's occupying too much of my mental real estate.

"Thanks, man. It was a helluva project, but worth it." Jake beams, proud as punch. But his words are background noise because my attention snaps back to Molly as she tucks a loose strand of hair behind her ear, her fingers delicate and precise.

"Dad would be proud," she says softly, and we all sober. Their dad might as well have been my own. I spent more time here at their house than I did my own parents' growing up. I remember the day I got the letter from Jake telling me of his heart attack.

"Yeah, he would have," I affirm, my voice sounding distant to my own ears.

My inner battle rages like a storm at sea. I'm caught between wanting to dive headfirst into whatever this thing with Molly could be and anchoring myself to the shore for Jake's sake. I mean, she's his sister. Off-limits should be my middle name, but the way she tilts her head when she laughs shreds my reservations to bits.

"Hey, Tanner, you're awfully quiet over there," Molly teases, her eyes twinkling like stars I've navigated by in darker times. "Lost at sea?"

"Something like that," I reply, forcing a laugh that

feels like it scrapes against my throat. It's not a total lie. I'm adrift alright, lost in the depth of her gaze.

"Thinking about your next adventure?" she probes gently, leaning forward ever so slightly, and the space between us feels charged with something electric.

"Maybe," I breathe out, and my words hang heavy in the room. There's truth there, an admission that goes beyond what I'm willing to explore.

I catch Jake's eye for a moment, searching for any sign that he sees through me, that he knows his best friend is dangerously close to crossing a line. But Jake just winks and turns to grab another round of beers from the fridge, clueless to the silent storm brewing inside me.

As I steal another glance at Molly, my eyes linger a touch too long on the curve of her lips, the gentle slope of her neck. And damn it, I want to taste every inch of that skin, map it out like uncharted territory.

"Tell me about the ocean," Molly whispers, almost as if she's reading my thoughts, her voice a siren's call.

And I'm thinking, *fuck it, let's drown.*

———

"Ah, c'mon Jake, you can't still be sore about the Great Water Balloon Siege of '09." I chuckle, lobbing a cushion at him to punctuate the tease, hoping it'll anchor me back to the present – back to the safety of old, uncomplicated times.

"Hey, that was strategic warfare!" Jake retorts, catching the cushion and tossing it back with a laugh that fills the room with warmth. "You're just lucky I didn't have my arsenal from college days."

"Sure, sure," I say, grinning despite the turmoil inside me. "Your Nerf collection really screams 'military genius.'"

Jake leans back, his hearty guffaws spreading across the room like wildfire, but even as I join in on the laughter, there's a part of me that isn't here, not really. It's caught up in a pair of deep brown eyes that seem to see right through me, drawing me in like gravity.

"Bro, focus. You're zoning out again!" Jake nudges me with his elbow, pulling me back from the brink of my Molly-induced trance.

"Sorry, man. Just... jet lag," I lie smoothly, or at least I hope it's smooth. My gaze flicks over to her, to Molly, and she's watching us with that knowing smile, like she sees straight past my bullshit excuses.

"Hey, how about that time we almost set the garage on fire?" I cut him off, desperate to steer this ship away from dangerous waters.

Jake launches into the story, animated and lively, and I try, God, do I try, to stay engaged. But every time Molly laughs, every time her hand brushes her hair back, I feel this electric jolt, this pull that's stronger than any riptide I've ever faced.

The evening stretches out before us, an endless sea of moments where I swim against the current of my own desire. I try to keep my eyes on Jake, on the safe harbor of our friendship, but they betray me, drifting over to Molly like she's the North Star guiding me home.

"Alright, I think I'm gonna turn in for the night," Molly eventually says, standing up and stretching gracefully, each movement poetry that writes itself onto the canvas of my mind. "It's been great catching up, Tanner."

"Yeah, likewise," I manage to get out, my voice rough like sandpaper as I watch her ascend the stairs, each step a siren song that chips away at my resolve.

"Damn," I mutter under my breath once she's out of earshot, running a hand through my hair.

"Everything alright?" Jake asks, eyes sharp with concern.

"Couldn't be better," I lie again, forcing a grin that feels more like a grimace. I stand up, clapping him on the shoulder. "I'm beat, too. Catch you in the morning?"

"Sure thing," he replies, oblivious to the storm raging inside me—the tempest of want and the heavy clouds of guilt.

I retreat to the guest room, feeling anything but

tired. As I lay in the dark, staring at the ceiling, I know sleep won't come easy tonight. Not with Molly's laughter echoing in my ears, not with her image burned into the backs of my eyelids.

Fuck, I'm in deep.

Molly

THE AIR IS thick with the scent of fresh produce as I meticulously inspect the apples, searching for that flawless one. The tangy smell of citrus from the nearby stand mingles in, promising refreshment and zest. My fingers are cool to the touch, brushing against the smooth skin of the fruits, but my mind's a million miles away.

Then, *he* walks in—the subject of my straying thoughts.

Tanner's presence shifts the atmosphere, like a storm rolling over calm seas. His footsteps are silent, but his aura screams across the room. And damn, does he wear those jeans well. He's not just a man. He's a walking call to attention, his very stance a testament to discipline and strength honed by years of military precision.

His gaze sweeps through the aisles like he's on a mission—which, knowing him, he probably is. His shopping list clutched in one hand, his focus is unyielding until his deep blue eyes land on me.

And there it is, the faintest upturn of his lips, that knowing smile that somehow manages to be both cocky and endearing.

Oh hell, my heart doesn't just skip a beat—it freaking somersaults. The warmth that floods my body is immediate and intense, like I've been doused with hot cocoa on a snowy day. I'm suddenly hyper-aware of every inch of myself, like I'm standing under a spotlight rather than the fluorescent lights of the grocery store.

Crap, I've been caught staring. Time to look busy. Real busy.

"Focus, Molly," I mutter under my breath, my cheeks burning with a blush that could rival any ripe tomato here. My fingers fumble for an apple, any apple, as if choosing the right one could shield me from his penetrating gaze.

"Perfect apple" becomes my mantra, but who am I kidding? The only perfection I'm really thinking about has got nothing to do with fruit and everything to do with the man who just walked into my orbit once again. Tanner, with his chiseled jawline that could cut glass and those biceps that suggest he could carry the world on his shoulders—or at least all of my groceries.

I snatch an apple, pretending it's the treasure I've been questing for, while my senses tingle with awareness of his approach. It's ridiculous, this game of cat and mouse we're playing among the avocados and bananas. But God, I don't want it to stop.

And then, oh my god, I realize Tanner's sauntering my way, each step brimming with the kind of confidence that comes from knowing you can handle any storm—or grocery store. He has this mischievous spark in his eyes, like he's up to no good, and I find myself hoping that I'm the cause of that twinkle.

"Hey there, Molly. Fancy meeting you here," he says, leaning casually against the mountain of avocados like he's auditioning for the role of 'grocery store heartthrob.'

I feel my eyes go wide, surprise flickering through me before it melts into amusement. A laugh bubbles out of me, unbidden, as if it's been tickled right out of my chest by his unexpected presence. "Well, Tanner, I guess it's just a lucky coincidence. Or maybe the universe is trying to tell us something." My cheeks are on fire, but I don't look away this time. I let him see the effect he has on me—let him see that I'm all in for whatever game we're playing.

Tanner's chuckle rumbles through the space between us, a sound that seems to vibrate right into my core, setting off all kinds of alarms—or maybe they're fireworks. He nods at my nearly overflowing basket, the one I've optimistically filled with ingredients for recipes I'll probably never attempt. "Need any help with those? I'm a pro at carrying heavy things, you know."

My pulse kicks up a notch, hammering against my ribcage as if it's trying to compete with the bass of a club anthem. It finds its rhythm there, fast and insistent. I hesitate, my gaze flicking to his outstretched hands—hands that look capable of lifting more than just a few grocery bags. There's strength in those fingers, a promise of steadiness and protection.

"Sure," I manage to say, the word escaping in a breathy exhale. I pass him the bags with the heaviest items—a testament to his past life where he's been honed by discipline and danger. It's just cans of soup and a bag of rice, but in his grasp, they seem like nothing.

We start walking towards the exit, and I can't stop myself from sneaking peeks at Tanner. His profile is sharp, each feature carved in a way that speaks of resilience and determination. The store lights catch in his dark hair, throwing shadows across his strong jawline, and damn, why does this feel like I'm living out some sort of sultry daydream?

"Watch your step," he says suddenly, his voice teasing yet laced with concern. I realize I'm about to collide with a stand of discounted chocolates, too caught up in my own head—and the sight of him—to notice. I sidestep it, mumbling a thanks, feeling the heat of embarrassment mingling with the warmth already swirling inside me.

I steal another glance, hoping I'm being subtle. His lips are quirked in an amused smile, as if he knows exactly what's going on in my mind. My stomach flips, doing an acrobatic routine worthy of a gold medal. Excitement jostles with nerves, a potent cocktail that has me both eager for and dreading the end of this unexpected encounter.

"Chocolates are a dangerous obstacle," he comments, eyes glinting with humor.

"Only to my waistline," I shoot back, finding my footing again in our easy banter.

His eyes fall to my waist, and my heart races. I can see the way his eyes trace over the slight curve of my waist and then stray down over my hips. My skin burns as if he physically traced my curves.

The automatic doors slide open with a whoosh, and we step into the liquid gold of late afternoon sunlight.

Tanner's arm brushes mine as he adjusts his grip on the bags, and I swear every nerve ending in my body fires at once.

"Long day?" he asks, turning that intense blue gaze on me. The kind that sees right through you.

"Um, yeah, sort of," I stammer, trying to look anywhere but at him. "You know, the usual hustle."

"Tell me about it." He nods, a lock of dark hair falling rebelliously across his forehead. "What's been keeping you busy?"

"Photography mostly," I say, finding my stride now. "I've got this crazy dream of traveling the world, capturing moments no one else sees."

"Sounds incredible," he replies, and there's a weight to his words, like they're more than just polite conversation filler.

"Thanks, it's..." I trail off, almost getting lost in those eyes again, before I snap back. "It's just a dream for now."

"Hey, dreams are good. They keep us moving forward," he says, and something about the way he says it—like he really means it—has warmth blooming in my chest.

"Exactly!" My enthusiasm bubbles over, and I can't help but share more. "There's so much beauty out there. I want to see it all—from the Eiffel Tower at sunset to the northern lights."

"Seeing the world through your lens must be something else," he murmurs, his expression suddenly serious.

My cheeks color. "You have no idea. Sometimes it feels like I'm stealing pieces of the universe, freezing them in time."

"Then you're quite the cosmic thief, Molly." His voice is low, a soft rumble that vibrates through me. "Can't say I don't admire that."

We reach my car, and I pop the trunk open, still riding the high from sharing my passion with someone as...magnetic as Tanner.

Tanner lifts the bags into the trunk with ease, the defined muscles of his arms flexing beneath his shirt—a subtle display of strength. Our fingers brush as he hands me the last bag, and damn, it's like a live wire zaps between us. My breath hitches, and I swear I can feel every nerve ending come alive.

"Thanks for helping me," I say, wondering how such simple words can feel so charged between us.

"Anytime," he replies, and I catch the promise in his eyes, an unspoken vow that sends another shiver skittering down my spine.

I catch him watching me with an intensity that should be too much but somehow isn't—not when it's him looking at me like I'm the most fascinating puzzle he's come across.

"Your view of the world—it's refreshing, Molly." His words are simple, but they resonate. "You've got this... innocence. Makes me want to see things through your lens."

"Is that so?" I tease, trying to keep the atmosphere light even though something heavy and thrilling settles in my chest. "Maybe one day you will."

"Maybe," he muses, and there's that promise again, hanging between us, alluring and unspoken.

"Molly," he says, and my name on his lips feels like a caress. "I've had a great time talking to you. I hope we can do this again sometime."

The sincerity in his gaze pins me in place, and I nod, words lodged in my throat. There's a gravity to his words, a silent acknowledgment that this isn't just idle chit-chat by the avocados. This is something else— something with a heartbeat.

"Absolutely," I breathe out, the words a little more than a whisper. Excitement buzzes through me like I'm a live wire, and it's all I can do to keep my knees from buckling under the weight of his gaze.

He steps closer, and I can almost count the shades of blue in his eyes before they close slightly, his face inching toward mine. "Until then, Molly," Tanner murmurs, his voice a seductive rumble that vibrates straight to my bones. The warmth of his breath tickles my ear, sending a cascade of goosebumps down my neck. And then his lips press softly against my cheek, a promise as much as a caress.

I'm frozen, breath hitched, as he pulls back. There's a slow burn where his mouth just was, an ache for more that blossoms in my chest. Tanner's smile is knowing, laced with a hint of danger, like he's well aware of the chaos he's stirring up inside me.

"Goodbye, Tanner," I manage, the world tilting a bit as he turns away. Goodbye? More like see you in every daydream for the foreseeable future.

"No," he shakes his head, his eyes darkening. "Never say goodbye to me, Molly. Not goodbye. Until later," he corrects.

I swallow, heat blossoming low in my belly. "Until later then."

I watch his retreating silhouette, a broad-shouldered shadow that etches itself into the canvas of my memory. Each step he takes is confident, sure—a rhythm that echoes in the suddenly too quiet space around me. My heart hammers a wild beat, and I press a hand to my chest, wondering if he can hear it too, like some kind of distress signal only he's tuned into.

"Wow," I mutter under my breath, the word dissolving in a laugh that bubbles up unbidden. This— the fluttering in my stomach, the heat on my cheeks— it's all new territory. And Tanner? He's the undisputed explorer, planting flags in parts unknown. I can still feel the ghost of his lips on my cheek, an imprint that sears through my skin and stirs something deep within me.

The cool metal of my car door handle grounds me for a second, a brief reprieve from the high I'm riding. I slide into the driver's seat, the leather familiar and comforting against my back. I'm half expecting the ignition to protest, to sense the seismic shift in me and refuse to start. But the engine purrs to life, obedient and unaware of the tectonic plates rearranging themselves beneath its wheels.

As I drive off, my smile's pretty much permanent, etched onto my face for the foreseeable future. The rearview mirror gives me a glimpse of the store fading away, but every cell in my body is keenly aware of where this road could lead. Hope blooms fierce in my chest, a wildflower stubborn in its will to grow.

I hope Tanner comes to visit my brother again tonight.

Tanner

I'M on my third set of push-ups, sweat dripping off my brow like a leaky faucet when my phone buzzes against the hardwood floor. The caller ID flashes Jake's name, and I hesitate, knowing that picking up means stepping into an emotional minefield I've been avoiding for days. But loyalty is a bitch with sharp teeth, and it bites hard. I answer with a grunt.

"Bro, where you been?" Jake's voice barrels through the line, casual as a Sunday morning.

"Been busy," I lie, pushing up into a sitting position and wiping my face with the back of my hand. Images of Molly, laughing in the cereal aisle with her hair cascading like a chocolate waterfall, flicker behind my eyelids. Damn, even the thought of her sends a twitch down to my groin. "What have you and Moll been up to?"

"I'm doing the same old shit, and Molly's got a date tonight with some guy named Leo."

His words slice through me. My hand tightens around my phone so hard I'm surprised I don't snap the fucking thing in two.

"Leo, huh?" My voice is a steady drawl, but inside, my stomach twists into a pretzel. "Good for her."

"What about you? What you been up to? Why haven't you dropped by the house lately?"

"Just busy taking care of some things, man," I lie again. I'm not in the mood for small talk. Not even with my best friend. Not when the reason for my sole existence has my entire body going up in flames right now.

"Hey, listen, man. Gotta go. Talk later?" I like to my best friend yet again.

"Sure. Don't be a stranger, okay?" Jake's concern is genuine, but it scrapes against nerves already frayed by longing and unspoken truths.

"Will do." I hang up, drop the phone, and let out a breath I didn't realize I was holding.

Alone again, I flop onto my back and pull my phone close, opening the app with Molly's smiling face staring back at me from the screen. I start scrolling through her posts, each photo and status update a breadcrumb leading me through the forest of her life. It's like a shot of adrenaline straight to the heart, seeing her smile, the way she throws her head back when she laughs, the glint of mischief in those big brown eyes.

I double-tap a picture of her at the beach, sunlight kissing her skin. My thumb hovers over the comment box before retreating. Can't leave any traces, not when I'm supposed to be keeping my distance.

I know it's crazy. I all but bit her head off and ordered her to never say goodbye to me that day I ran into her at the store.

And then I fucking ghosted her. But I had to. My feelings are already so intense. I know there's no way in hell I'm going to be able to be in the same room as her with her brother without him being able to pick up on my feelings. It's all I can do to keep my hands off her when I'm near her. I can't stop my eyes from adoring her. All I need is for her brother—my best friend—to see the lustful way I leer at his little sister.

But damn, if I would have know staying away would prompt her to go on a date. My stomach roils again.

"Who the hell is this Leo?" The question punches out of me, jealousy coiling tight in my chest. I find a post with his name tagged, and there he is—Mr. Perfect with his sandy blonde hair and smirk that says he knows just how charming he is. I bet he doesn't even have to try not to come in his pants when he sees her.

"Damn it," I curse under my breath, hating the heat that flushes my cheeks and the way my heart races like I'm back in the thick of a mission with everything on the line. But this isn't about survival. This is about desire, raw and relentless, clawing its way out of the shadows.

I chuck the phone aside and force myself to stand, muscles screaming for release, mind warring with itself. I need to get out, run until my legs give out, or hit something until the fire in my veins turns to ice.

But as I lace up my boots, I know I'm only running from the inevitable. Molly has seeped into my bones, and no amount of space or silence will cleanse her from my system.

I'm posted up across the street from the coffee shop, a ball cap pulled low over my eyes. It's my third day tailing Molly, and with every passing hour, I feel like I'm walking a razor's edge between protective and pathetic. She steps out, that brunette hair of hers catching the morning sun in a way that makes my chest tighten. A laugh breaks free from her lips, and it's like a punch to the gut—I want her to laugh like that around me.

Only me.

"Focus, damn it," I mutter to myself, watching as she walks down the sidewalk, blissfully unaware of my presence. My hands grip the steering wheel until my knuckles turn white. I tell myself it's just to make sure she's safe, that some part of me is still the SEAL who watches over his own. But another part, the one that's all raw edges and dark corners, whispers that I'm full of shit.

She pauses at a bookstore window, peering at the display, and my phone buzzes. It's Jake. I let it ring twice before I pick up.

"Hey, man," Jake says, his voice all easy charm and brotherly warmth. "You're still MIA. What's going on?"

"Nothing much, just keeping busy," I reply, my gaze never leaving Molly as she continues down the street. My voice has that flat tone I can't seem to shake these days.

"Busy with what?" He probes, but I deflect with a vague mention of errands and workouts—anything to steer him away from the truth.

"Sure," he says, but there's a hesitation that tells me he's not buying it. "We should hang out soon, though. You, me, a couple of beers? Like old times."

"Sounds good," I say, even though every cell in my

body screams that being around him, around *her*, is the last thing I need. "Let's set it up."

The call ends, but that sense of disconnection lingers. I watch Molly disappear into a store, and I'm already calculating how long she'll be, where she'll head next. It's a routine now, this shadow dance of mine.

"Shit," I curse under my breath. This isn't me.

Or maybe it's exactly me, and that's the problem. The lines are blurring, and I'm losing sight of where Tanner the friend ends and Tanner the obsessed begins. And the worst part? I can't seem to find it in me to stop.

I'm nursing a beer at the corner of Jake's couch when he slumps down next to me, his brow furrowed in that brotherly concern I've seen a million times. The game blares on the TV, but neither of us is watching. There's a tension in the air, thick enough to slice through.

"Man, you're about as jumpy as a cat in a room full of rocking chairs," Jake says, eyeing me like I'm a puzzle he's determined to solve. "Spill it, T. You've been dodging my calls, blowing off plans. That's not like you."

"Jake, I'm fine," I insist, forcing a laugh. It sounds

hollow even to my own ears. "Honestly, just working through some things. You know, the whole 'adjusting to civilian life' dance."

He's quiet for a moment, studying me with those sharp eyes that miss nothing. "Adjusting, huh? Because from where I'm sitting, it looks like you're gearing up for another covert op."

"Wouldn't you like to know?" I quip, trying to deflect with humor. But my grin feels like a mask that's starting to crack.

"Damn right, I would." He punches my arm lightly, but there's an undercurrent of seriousness that wasn't there before. "You're my best friend, Tanner. If something's eating at you, I want to help."

"Appreciate it, man, but it's just personal stuff. Gotta figure it out on my own," I say, taking a long pull from the bottle. The bitterness of the hops mirrors the taste in my mouth when I lie to him.

"Personal stuff," he echoes, nodding slowly. But then he leans in, his voice dropping to a conspiratorial whisper. "Is it a woman?"

"Jesus, Jake," I choke on the beer, coughing and sputtering as I try to regain my composure, praying he isn't on to me.

"Hey, I call it like I see it," he shoots back with a smirk. "And I see you, brother. Something—or rather someone— has got you wound tighter than a two-dollar watch. So, spill. Who is she? Where'd you meet her?"

"Alright, Dr. Phil," I grumble, setting the beer down with a little more force than necessary. "Thanks for the session, but I've got it under control."

"Sure, sure." He backs off, but his look tells me he's not convinced. "Just remember, I'm here if you need to talk. No judgments."

"Got it." I nod, grateful for the out even as guilt twists inside me. "Now, can we focus on the game before we miss something epic?"

"Fine by me," he agrees, but there's a flicker of concern still lingering in his gaze.

If he only knew the half of it…

———

I'm hunched over my laptop, the hum of the machine a dull companion to the clicking of keys as I refresh Molly's profile for what must be the twentieth time in an hour. My fingers pause mid-stroke, my breath catching as a new photo pops up. There she is, laughing with that wide-eyed innocence that punches me right in the gut. She's at the local coffee shop, her caption a cheerful quip about caffeine kicks.

"Damn," I mutter under my breath, the word a mix of admiration and frustration.

I close the laptop with a snap, my decision made. I can't just sit here, stalking her through a screen. I need eyes on her—real, live, breathing-in-the-same-air eyes. It's not enough to know she's okay. I have to see it, reassure myself she's safe and sound. And maybe, just maybe, get my fix of those brown eyes and that smile.

Throwing on a hoodie that does little to conceal my build but plenty to blend into the crowd, I head out the door. The crisp air hits me like a splash of cold water, but it doesn't cool the heat coiling tight in my core. I jog down the street, a purposeful stride taking me toward the heart of town.

I spot the familiar sign of the coffee shop swinging gently in the breeze. Slowing down, I scan the area, my SEAL training kicking in despite the mundanity of the task. Not that watching over Molly ever feels mundane. It feels necessary—like breathing.

There she is, perched at a table outside, her laughter reaching me across the distance. It's like music, stirring things inside me that have no business waking up. I duck behind a newspaper stand, my gaze locked on her. She's animated, her hands moving in the air as she talks to a friend. Safe. Happy.

"Christ," I breathe out, the tension easing from my shoulders even as my heart races double-time.

I should walk away, melt back into the shadows and leave her to her life that doesn't include me. But my feet are traitors, edging closer until I can hear the lilt of her voice, catch the scent of her shampoo carried on the wind.

"Can I help you find something?" a chipper voice asks, and I turn to face the barista who's popped up beside me like a jack-in-the-box.

"Uh, yeah." My voice is gruff, the words tumbling out. "One of those chocolate croissant thingies, to go."

I fork over the cash without haggling and beat a hasty retreat, pastry in hand and heart lodged firmly in my throat.

Fuck I've got it bad. And by God, if this isn't the most reckless mission I've ever taken on.

Tanner

I'M PERCHED like a damn bird of prey outside her window, the one veiled by those sheer curtains that tease and reveal just enough to torment me. I watch as she dabs on eyeshadow that makes her big brown eyes pop. She's all focused, sticking out her tongue just a bit as she concentrates—it's cute as hell. Now she's rifling through her closet, fabrics fluttering in her hands until she settles on something that hugs her petite figure like it's made for her. A pang of jealousy bites at me. I didn't even know I could feel like this—possessive and raw.

I watch her smooth down the skirt of her dress and

there's this tightness in my chest, hot and uncomfortable.

The restaurant they pick is one of those swanky joints with mood lighting so dim you can barely see your hand in front of your face, and the music—a soft, jazzy number—is just loud enough to make leaning closer a necessity. Damn strategic, if you ask me.

They're seated at a corner table, and Leo's giving her that smile. You know the one, the "I'm not just interested in your hobbies" kind. He leans in, earnest, nodding as she talks about her photography. She's gesturing with her hands, all animated, while he's throwing out words like 'composition' and 'lighting'—like he knows what he's talking about. But here's the kicker—he actually does. And she's soaking it up, laughing at his jokes, flipping that brunette hair over her shoulder.

"Your framing is exceptional, Molly. Have you ever thought about doing a gallery showing?" Leo asks, voice dripping with encouragement.

"Really? Do you think they're good enough?" Her cheeks flush with the compliment, and it's clear she values his opinion. My jaw clenches.

"Absolutely. With your eye? People would be blown away."

He's slick, I'll give him that. Watching them, I feel words clawing up my throat, desperate for release, but

I force them back down. I'm a SEAL for God's sake, a master of control. Yet here I am, ready to blow a gasket over my best friend's little sister.

My knuckles go white, gripping the edge of the bar like a lifeline. From my vantage point across the room, I watch them, my jaw set so tight it aches. Molly's laugh trickles through the clink of glasses and the low hum of dinner conversations, a sound I realize I'm starving for. It's like a shot to the chest, seeing her light up under Leo's attention.

"More wine, sir?" The bartender's question is white noise, drowned out by the blood thundering in my ears.

I shake my head. Can't risk dulling my senses—not when every fiber of my being is strung tight, coiled like a spring. I should be over there, not him. I should be the one making her smile, damn it.

As her hand brushes his arm, something snaps inside me. It feels like I'm watching this all unfold from outside my body, some screwed-up out-of-body experience where I see myself losing it bit by bit.

I push away from the bar. My legs move with a mind of their own. I'm aware of heads turning, eyes following the pissed-off giant cutting through the restaurant.

Let them stare.

"Hey!" My voice booms as I reach their table, the word slicing through the soft music like a gunshot.

Leo—fucking Leo, the little bag of shit—swivels in his seat, green eyes wide, the surprise etched on his face clear even to someone half-blind. Molly's mouth falls open, her eyes mirroring his shock, but it's him I focus on.

"Can I help you, man?" Leo's tone is cautious, a hint of confusion threading through the politeness.

"What do you think you're doing?" I growl, looming over him, my shadow swallowing their table. My eyes lock onto him, willing him to understand that this isn't a friendly chat.

"Whoa, Tanner, what's going on?" Molly's voice cuts through the tension, but it's like I'm trapped in a tunnel, her words echoing around me.

I ignore her for a moment, because right now it's about him and me, and this dance we're doing where only one of us walks away unscathed.

"Back off," I snarl at Leo, close enough now that he has to crane his neck to hold my gaze.

"Okay, okay, just calm down," he says, hands raised in a gesture of surrender. "We're just talking—"

"Talking, huh?" I spit the word out like it tastes bad. "You get your kicks chatting up other guys' girls?"

"Tanner—" Molly starts, but I interrupt her, unable to contain the storm raging inside me.

"Let's go, Molly. *Now*." My command brooks no argument, each syllable hammered out with precision.

Leo stands, looking between the two of us, trying to read the room. He doesn't stand a chance. With my frame blocking out the rest of the world, I'm all he sees —a living, breathing warning sign.

"Sure, man. No problem here," he says, backing down as everyone in the restaurant watches.

I reach for Molly's hand, and though she hesitates, those big brown eyes flickering with a torrent of emotions, she takes it. Her fingers are cool and small in mine, yet they sear my skin like a brand.

"You're coming with me," I tell her.

***

Molly

My heart skips erratically as Tanner's deep blue eyes lock onto mine, a storm brewing within them. Is it fucked up that I find this all extremely…hot?

And Tanner called me his girl…

Whoa…just whoa.

It's happening, right here in the middle of a

crowded restaurant—Tanner's raw jealousy laid bare for all to see, including me.

And I couldn't be more turned on.

"Tan, it's not what you think," I try to explain, but my voice is barely audible over the thunderous beat of my pulse.

He's close now, so close I can feel the heat radiating from his body. I'm momentarily lost in the intensity of his gaze, that inexplicable pull towards him stronger than ever. It's an attraction that I've tried to tamp down, to ignore, but it simmers there, always just beneath the surface.

"Come on." His hand wraps around mine, firm and insistent.

"Wait, Tanner, listen—" I attempt once more, my wide eyes pleading for understanding.

"Later," he says curtly, tugging me gently with him.

I allow him to pull me from the restaurant. As we weave through the tables, I feel every eye on us, but most acutely, I feel Tanner—his presence enveloping me, protective and overwhelming.

It hits me then, the realization piercing through the confusion—Tanner thinks I'm on a date with Leo. He doesn't know this was just supposed to be a business meeting. A laugh bubbles up inside me, tinged with hysteria. Of all the ways I imagined Tanner might finally show he cared, causing a scene wasn't one of them.

And yet, despite the madness of the situation, part of me thrills at the possessiveness in his actions. Tanner, my brother's best friend, the former Navy SEAL with walls I've never been able to scale, is staking his claim on me in front of everyone. It's wrong, it's outrageous, but God, it's also a little bit exhilarating.

The cool night air nips at my skin as we exit the restaurant, the heated tension between us making me almost immune to the chill. The city lights blur into streaks of color as we stride down the sidewalk, Tanner's grip on my hand both a lifeline and an anchor.

"Where are we going?" My breath fogs in front of me, the question hanging there like my own personal cloud.

"Back to my place." His voice is a low rumble, a sound that seems to vibrate through me.

My heart hammers against my ribs, each beat screaming this is insane, but every fiber of my being is pulled taut with anticipation. This isn't just about escaping the prying eyes back at the restaurant. It's about us, about the unresolved tension that's been building since...well, since forever.

We don't talk as we walk, the silence thick with words unspoken. Every step feels charged, heavy with the weight of our mutual desire. I'm keenly aware of every brush of his fingers against mine, the solid warmth of him beside me. It's as if my whole body is straining towards him, a magnet drawn to its opposite pole.

We finally reach his apartment, the familiar exterior now seeming like a foreign land, promising unknown adventures. He unlocks the door and ushers me inside where the dim lighting casts shadows that dance across his chiseled features.

"Nice place," I say, though I wouldn't give a damn if he'd taken me to a beat-up old shoe box. So long as I'm with him.

"Thanks." He closes the door behind us, and the soft click sounds like the starting gun of a race.

I can feel the energy buzzing between us, nearly tangible in the semi-darkness. There's a moment where we just stand there, drinking each other in, the air practically humming with the current that's crackling in the space narrowing between us.

His gaze locks onto mine, those deep blue eyes that always seem to see right through me, now darkened with something fierce and raw. And in that look, I see it all—the jealousy, the frustration, the thinly veiled hunger.

"God, Molly..." He steps closer, his voice a growl that sends shivers skittering down my spine.

"Tanner," I whisper, my own voice betraying the whirlwind of emotions I'm trying to contain.

Our glances are no longer fleeting—they're lingering, heavy, full of silent promises and unspoken confessions. The air is thick with the scent of possibility, and I find myself inching toward him, unable to resist the pull any longer.

We're a hair's breadth apart now, and the electricity is undeniable. Every nerve ending feels alive, every breath shared, every inch of space between us charged with the anticipation of what might happen next.

I think about how confused I've been the past few days. How it hurt when he stayed away from me after that day at the supermarket. I know why he did it without him even telling me. This, us, it's complicated. He's my brother's best friend.

He must read it all in my eyes because he murmurs, "I'm sorry, baby. I know. I tried to stay away, but I couldn't."

And just like that, all is forgiven. I don't know what comes over me, but I surge forward, closing the final inch between us, and it's like striking a match, igniting the pent-up yearning that's been smoldering between Tanner and me. My hands find his shoulders, gripping hard muscle, as his arms wrap around me, pulling me into the solid wall of his chest.

"Been wanting to do this since the moment I set

eyes on you," he growls against my lips before claiming them in a kiss that sears straight through to my soul. His mouth moves over mine with a possessive urgency, and I moan, lost in the raw intensity of it. It's hungry, it's fierce—it's everything I've fantasized about and more.

Tanner's hands roam down my back, branding me with his touch, pushing any last shred of restraint out of the window. Our bodies press together, leaving no secrets unexplored as clothes are shed in a feverish rush. Skin on skin, we're a tangle of limbs and whispered names, each caress dialing up the heat until we're nothing but pure sensation and need.

"Tell me you want this," he pants, eyes blazing into mine, demanding affirmation.

"God, yes," I gasp, arching against him, "I want you—all of you."

That's all it takes. He lifts me effortlessly, our mouths never parting, and carries me to the bedroom where we fall onto the bed in a cascade of limbs and lust.

"Look at you," he praises me as his eyes sweep over my naked body. "You're fucking perfect, Molly."

My eyes sweep over his chiseled muscles, drinking him in. I reach out and lightly rake my fingertips over his hard chest, and I see him visibly shudder.

His cock juts out from between his thighs, and I swallow, suddenly nervous if it will fit.

I'm not an idiot. I know how sex works, but I'm still a virgin, and Tanner is *not* small.

"I-I'm a virgin," I blurt out.

He stills, his blue eyes locking with mine.

And then he starts breathing heavily. His nostrils flare, and his hands fist in the sheets as if it's taking everything in him to control himself.

"Shouldn't have told me that, baby. I'm already dying for you, but now that know I'm going to be the first one—the *only* one—inside you. Fuck, sweetheart, I might nut myself right here."

"Tanner," I whisper his name.

And then his lips crash onto mine. A growl escapes his throat, and every inch of him presses against me.

The kiss is sloppy, possessive, and I love it. His hands roam my body, molding me to him as he begins to move his hips against mine. I moan into the kiss as an intense heat pools between my thighs.

"I need to be inside you, Molly, so fucking bad. Tell me now if you don't want this. Tell me while I still have a shred of control left."

I shake my head. "I want this too. I trust you, Tanner."

He growls, and then he's no longer being gentle. He slams home inside me, filling me to the hilt. I bite back a moan of pain as he stretches me, his cock hitting something deep inside of me that makes the pain turn to pleasure.

"Fuck, sorry, Molly," he pants, stilling inside me, but I don't want him to stop.

"It's okay. Don't stop."

He moans low in approval before he starts to move again, slowly at first but then faster and faster until our bodies are slapping together. His grip on my hips tightens, and I can feel him dragging himself deeper and deeper within me with each thrust, hitting a spot inside me that has me seeing stars.

"Oh, fuck, Tanner, yes," I mewl, my back arching off the bed as an incredible feeling starts to build within my core. "Don't stop."

This is what all fuss is about, I think just as Tanner buries himself deep inside me one last time. I feel my first-ever orgasm detonate throughout my body, leaving me dizorientated and breathless in its wake.

"God, I love you," he growls as he starts to come inside me. I feel his hot liquid spurting inside me and then running out between my legs.

He collapses on top of me, and we lay there, a tangled mess of sweaty limbs and racing hearts. I can barely piece together a coherent thought. But one thing cuts through the fog of post-bliss daze.

Tanner said he loves me.

Even as my body still tingles from the aftershocks, my mind starts racing ahead. This complicates things—my brother will flip when he finds out—but right now, I don't care. I'm too consumed by the thrill of having Tanner's arms around me, of feeling wanted and desired in a way I've never felt before.

"I love you too," I confess.

Tanner's pupils dilate before he covers my lips with his own again and resumes moving his still-hard cock inside me. "Gonna fuck you again, baby. I'm sorry. I got to. Gotta make sure this pussy knows it's mine. Only mine. You're never going to have another man inside you like this. Do you understand?"

My body thrills at his possessive words, my pussy clenching tight around him in response as he saws in and out of me again, his intense gaze poring into my eyes with something that borders on madness.

"Yes," I confirm. "Yours."

"I mean it, Molly," he growls. "No other man touches you. No one looks at you. No one comes near you." He fucks me harder to punctuate each demand until I'm screaming 'yes!' over and over again.

I love his demands. I love his possessiveness.

If this is what it means to be his, then sign me the fuck up.

CHAPTER
FIVE

Tanner

I'M LEANING against the kitchen counter when the back door clicks open. My pulse revs up, a familiar thrill coursing through me as she slips inside. "Hey," Molly whispers, that mischievous sparkle in her big brown eyes making my heart skip.

"Hey yourself," I murmur, closing the space between us with a couple of strides. My hands find the small of her back, pulling her close. She's warmth and all the home comforts I've been craving rolled into one petite, beautiful package.

Our lips crash together, no hellos needed, just this— raw and real. The kiss deepens, our tongues tangoing with a hunger that feels like it's been building for lifetimes. Every touch is fire, every breath shared.

She's my other half.

"Missed you," she breathes out, her fingers tracing the line of my jaw, down to the dog tags that still hang around my neck.

"Every second," I promise, meaning every damn word. We're a tangle of limbs and need, right here in my kitchen, where any of my nosy neighbors could peer through a window and spot us. But risk has become part of the taste of her, and I can't get enough.

"Got something for you," I say, pulling back just enough to see the question in her eyes. The corners of her mouth lift in a smile that nearly knocks me sideways every time.

"Is it food?" she teases, because she knows me, knows the way to my own heart is through my stomach, just like hers.

"Better," I say with a wink, leading her by the hand. I guide her out the back, to where the night has laid out a blanket of stars above us. There's a real blanket spread on the grass, and I've filled a basket with everything Molly loves—chocolate-covered strawberries, a Caprese salad with that fancy mozzarella she adores, and a bottle of sparkling cider because she's got class.

"Wow," she gasps, stepping onto the blanket and looking around at the fairy lights I've strung up in the trees. It's no SEAL mission, but planning this gave me the same adrenaline rush, more actually because it was for *her*.

"Only the best for you," I say, proud as hell of the setup. We settle down, the evening air just crisp enough to make her snuggle closer. I pop the cork on the cider, pour us each a glass, and we cheer. "To us," I say, because there's no one else in this picture. Not now, not ever.

We feed each other bites, laughter mingling with the soft rustling of leaves. Her laugh is a melody I'd recognize anywhere, light and free, undoing the knots inside me piece by piece.

"Did you cook all this yourself?" she asks, eyebrow raised in playful skepticism.

"Hey, I can navigate a kitchen. Mostly," I admit, grinning. We eat, talk about everything and nothing, and I thank whatever fates have let me have this—her company, her smile, her.

I'm a lucky bastard.

As dinner winds down, the candles flicker and the stars seem to shine just for us. Every glance she throws my way is charged with that sweet tension that promises more—so much more. And I'm ready to give her everything under this endless sky, just so long as she keeps looking at me like that.

I pull Molly into my arms, our sides molding

together like two pieces meant to fit. She exhales softly, her breath a warm whisper against the nape of my neck.

"Look at that one," she murmurs, pointing up. I follow her finger to a twinkling light dancing in the dark sea overhead.

"Shooting star," I say. "Make a wish."

She squeezes my hand, her eyes reflecting the cosmos. "I already have everything I want right here."

Her words hang in the air, more intimate than a whisper, more binding than a vow. I tighten my hold on her, urgency swelling within me as I gaze down into those deep brown eyes that don't just see me—they understand me.

"Molly," My voice is thick with emotion. "You've gotta know something. I've been through hell and back, but you... you make it all worth it. I meant it when I said I love you. Those weren't just words said in a moment of passion. There's no one else who makes me feel...alive." It's more than a confession. It's the raw truth of my heart.

Her lips part in a silent gasp, and then she's kissing me, soft and sweet and slowly stoking the fire inside me until there's nothing left but need—pure and blazing.

"Love you too, Tanner. So much," she whispers between kisses that grow hungrier, deeper.

And then we're a tangle of limbs and desire as passion ignites between us. I'm not gentle—I can't be—not with the way she's clawing at my back, urging me on. "Fuck, Molly, I need you," I groan, pressing her into the blanket beneath us.

"Then take me. I'm yours," she breathes out, her voice laced with that delicious edge of innocence that drives me wild.

My hands roam over her body, worshiping every curve and dip, every soft sigh and sharp intake of breath only making my cock harder. I'm leaking precum all over the place, the side of my shaft slimy with the evidence of my desire for her.

I peel away her clothes with hurried movements, exposing her to the night air and to my hungry gaze. Her skin is moonlit perfection, begging for my touch.

"God, you're beautiful," I rasp, as I trail kisses down her collarbone, savoring the salt of her skin.

"More, Tanner...please," she begs, and I oblige, sinking into her warmth. The world narrows down to the slick heat of her, the clutch of her fingers in my hair, the way she moves against me—frenzied and free.

"She cries out as I thrust into her.

"Fuck!" I growl as I set a pace that's both punishing and perfect. Our bodies move together in a wild rhythm, each stroke driving us closer to that edge, that sweet abyss of pleasure.

"Say my name," I order her. "Let me hear who you belong to when you come all over my cock."

She pants, her nails digging into my shoulders.

"Come on, gorgeous," I urge her. "I'm almost there."

"Tanner!" she screams as she comes apart under me, her climax triggering my own. I'm lost in the rush, the intensity, the connection that's so damn much more than physical.

We lie there afterward, hearts racing, still joined as we catch our breaths under the stars.

This is more than a stolen moment.

This is *everything*.

I pull Molly closer. Our sweat mingles, the scent of us—a heady perfume of love and lust—wraps around me like a blanket. I press my lips to her forehead, whispering words meant only for her ears.

"Stay with me," I murmur against her skin, each beat of my heart spelling out her name. "Forever."

"Always," she breathes back, her fingers tracing lazy circles on my chest. Her smile is tired but blissful, a perfect reflection of the satiation that hums through my veins.

We're pieces of a puzzle that fit only in the dark, away from prying eyes. Away from Jake—her brother and my best friend.

It's a dangerous game we're playing—Jake's trust

hanging by a thread, our future uncertain—but damn if it doesn't feel worth every risk.

Molly must be thinking the same thing becuase she begins, "My brother..." Her voice trembles as she trails off without finishing her sentence.

"I know," I say simply. "Let's not think about that now. Let's just be here, together."

"Okay," she whispers, sealing the promise with a kiss so tender it could break hearts.

My arms tighten around her, and I can't help it. I realize that I'm willing to throw everything away—my friendship with Jake, my life, hell even my soul— for her.

———

The days drag like a rudderless ship lost at sea. Every second apart from Molly is an exercise in restraint, a battle against the tide of desire that threatens to pull me under. I catch glimpses of her across town, our eyes locking in a silent conversation that leaves my skin tingling with anticipation. At the café, her laughter spills over the rim of her coffee cup, a sound that stirs something deep within my chest.

She texts, and I can almost hear her voice, see the curve of her lips as she types.

Missed you.

Counting the minutes.

I pocket my phone with a grin that doesn't quite reach my eyes. It's torture, this waiting game, but every stolen touch, every secretive smile we share is fuel on the fire of my longing.

I realize I can't be with her everyday. Not if we're going to keep this hidden from Jake.

But fuck it, I can't stay away from her. I've waited long enough.

Once it's night, I climb up the trellis to her window. The cool metal bites into my palms, but the thrill of seeing Molly, of being near her, fuels my ascent.

I slip through the open window with practiced silence, a skill honed from years in the military now repurposed for clandestine trysts with the girl who owns my soul.

"Jesus, you scared me," she hisses, but her wide-eyed surprise gives way to a mischievous grin. "What are you doing here?"

"Can't stay away," I confess, my breath hitching as her nightgown slides to reveal creamy thighs in the moonlight. "Needed you."

"Tanner," she hisses, "Jake is right down the hall!"

But her hands are already tugging at my shirt, pulling me into the warmth of her room—and her bed.

"Then you better be quiet," I growl as I capture her mouth with mine. The kiss is a match to kerosene, and my entire body goes up in flames as her tiny tongue licks into my mouth.

My hands are pulling at her nightie, my cock already poking out of my pants.

The danger of discovery adds an edge to every caress, every gasp. Jake's presence down the hall isn't enough to quell the storm we stir in each other. If anything, it fans the flames.

"Touch me, Tanner," she moans into my ear, and I oblige with a fervor that borders on reverence. Every curve and valley of her body is a terrain I'll never tire of exploring.

"Like that?" I ask, even as I know the answer. Her body arches, seeking more.

"Fuck, yes!" Her response is a litany of whispered pleasure that echoes off the walls. We move with abandon, chasing the high that comes with stolen moments, with forbidden love.

"Tan..." Her voice breaks on my name, a plea that I answer with every fiber of my being.

I thrust inside her and cover her mouth with my

hand to muffle the scream that erupts from her. "Ssh," I hush her even as my cock shoots precum inside her.

She whimpers as I start to pound into her, and I swear I'm harder than I've ever been in my entire life.

"You like that, don't you?" I ask you. "Like getting your pussy pounded hard with your brother right down the hall, don't you?"

She whimpers again, her eyes rolling back in her head as her orgasm rocks through it.

"Fucking shit!" I whisper yell as my own climax hits me. I feel the seed rushing from my balls and up my stalk, and I plant myself deep inside her just as it spurts from my tip and into her waiting hot box.

We're playing with fire, Molly and I. But as she drifts off to sleep in my arms, her trust pressing heavy against my chest, I can't help but think some things are worth getting burned for.

CHAPTER
SIX

Tanner

"OH FUCK, baby, you keep that up I'm going to come." I'm driving into Molly's sweet cunt like there's no tomorrow, my balls coiled tight. Her pussy is fluttering around me. She's mewling and purring like a little kitten.

And then I hear the door bang open.

I look over and Jake's standing there like a deer in headlights, eyes popping out of his skull. "What the actual—"

"Jake!" I bark out his name, my heart slamming against my ribs. This is about as far from ideal as it gets. Molly's beneath me, her brown eyes wide with shock, our clothes scattered like confetti after New Year's Eve.

"Jesus, Tanner!" Jake's face is a masterpiece of rage, painted in shades of red I didn't even know existed. He throws up a hand to shield his eyes, but not before firing off a string of curses that would make a sailor blush. And believe me, I know sailors.

"Man, I—" Words are useless, little grenades that fail to launch as I scramble to salvage what's left of dignity and decency in the room.

"Get the hell out!" he roars, his voice a sledge-hammer smashing through whatever flimsy explana-tion I'm trying to piece together. Jake's always been the laidback type—until you cross a line. And damn, have I crossed it.

"Jake, this isn't—" How do I even finish that sentence? This isn't what it looks like? Because, hell, it's exactly what it looks like.

Instinct finally takes over. I grab the sheet and yank it over Molly, my palm flat against the mattress as I pivot to shield her with my body. The cold air hits my skin, but the heat from Jake's glare might as well be a blowtorch.

"Talk, Tanner, or so help me God, I'll end you," Jake spits through gritted teeth, his fists balled up at his sides like he's ready to go a few rounds.

"Look, this is not—"

"Save it!" His voice booms, cutting me off. "I trusted you, man! You're supposed to be my brother, not some creep who pounces on my sister!"

"Jake, I would never—" My throat's sandpaper dry, words tumbling out in a clumsy jumble. "It's not like that."

My best friend's eyes are still murderous, though, and for good reason. He literally just caught me banging his little sister. It's a wonder I'm not dead already. I know how protective Jake is of his litter sister, especially after their parents died and he took on the responsibility of acting like Molly's parental figure.

"Jake, man, listen to me," I start, my voice gravelly with urgency. "I love your sister. More than anything."

The words hang heavy in the air, an anchor thrown in the midst of a tempest. Jake's eyes, twin infernos of betrayal and fury, bore into mine. But it's the truth, raw and bare, like a nerve exposed.

"Love her?" His laughter is sharp, bitter. "You have a hell of a way of showing it, Tanner!"

"Please." It's a plea, straight from the gut. "I can't imagine life without Molly. I never meant to hurt you or betray your trust."

"Tanner," Molly whispers from behind me, her voice quivering like a plucked string. I can feel her hand trembling against my back, unsure whether to push or pull.

"Just go," she commands, louder now. The two words hit like a punch to the chest. Her face is a storm of emotions—embarrassment, pain, love—all swirling together until they're indistinguishable.

"Baby, don't—" I try, but she cuts me off with a look that breaks my heart.

"Go, Tanner. Now." There's steel in her voice, a resolve that makes my heart hammer against my ribs.

I shake my head. "No, I'm not going anywhere without you. We're in this together, remeber?" There's no way I'm leaving her to face her brother's wrath alone. Not that I think Jake would hurt her. Just that's not in me. I don't run.

Her eyes plead with me, big and brimming, but I won't be swayed.

I square my shoulders and turn to face Jake.

Christ, his fists are bunched so tight they're shaking. The veins on his neck stand out like cords, his face red as a stop sign. Jake, my best friend, looks ready to tear me apart with his bare hands.

"You think you can just waltz in here, mess around with my sister, and what? Just walk away?"

My heart's pounding, adrenaline sparking through me. Old instincts kick in, ones I thought I'd buried when I left the Navy. But I don't want to fight him. Not Jake.

"Damn it, Jake!" I shout, trying to break through to him. "I love her!"

He doesn't budge, doesn't blink, just stands there, coiled and ready. And that's when I know what I have to do. Before I can second-guess myself, I drop to one knee.

"Jake," I start again, my voice rough around the edges, "Molly, I'm not leaving here without making one thing clear."

My hand reaches into my pocket, fingers closing around the tiny velvet box I've been carrying for weeks. My heart's doing double time, but when I look up at Molly, everything else fades out. She's my beacon, my true north.

"Molly," I say, loud enough to cut through the tension, "will you marry me?"

Silence crashes down like an avalanche. Even Jake's breath catches, the sound loud in the sudden stillness. There's no script for moments like this, no playbook or SOP to follow. Just raw, unscripted life, hanging on the edge of a single question.

Molly's face is a picture I can't quite read. It's like she's flipped through every emotion in the book and landed on a page that's blank. Her lips part, but no sound comes out. She's still wrapped in a sheet just staring at me, those big brown eyes wide as saucers.

"Tanner," she finally breathes, her voice so faint it

could be mistaken for the breeze. "What are you doing?"

I stay there, on one knee, my heart hammering against my ribs like it's trying to escape. I've seen combat, stared down the barrel of a gun with less fear than I feel right now. But this, right here with Molly, is the bravest thing I've ever done.

"Making the biggest bet of my life," I say, hoping my grin doesn't look as shaky as it feels. "C'mon, Mol. Roll the dice with me."

Jake's still standing there, his hands slowly uncurling from fists to slack-jawed disbelief. His gaze cuts between us like he's watching a tennis match from hell. "Are you out of your freaking mind?" he explodes, almost a whisper, almost a shout.

"Quite possibly," I admit, my focus never leaving Molly's face. I need her to see how much I mean this, how much she means to me. "But I'm crazy about your sister, man."

"Jesus, Tanner..." Jake rakes a hand through his hair, looking like he wishes it were my neck instead. His eyes narrow, flickering with something dark and stormy. Protective instincts are battling it out with whatever soft spot he has for seeing Molly happy.

"Jake, please—" Molly starts, her voice quivering with a cocktail of hope and anxiety.

"Shut up, Mol," Jake snaps, but there's no bite to it.

He's torn, I can tell. Love does that to you. Splits you right down the middle and makes you question which half is right.

"Look, I know this is... unconventional," I push on, the ring burning a hole in my palm. "And I get why you're pissed. But she's it for me, Jake."

He looks like he might charge at me, or maybe have a stroke. I can't tell which.

"Say something, Molly," I urge softly, turning back to her. "Before your brother actually kills me."

Her mouth moves, but no words come out. I can see the war inside her too—want versus should, heart versus head. But love, I know, love can win any war if you let it.

Time stretches into a tightrope, thin and quivering under the weight of our stares. Jake's features are chiseled from stone—anger, shock, love all mashed together in that rugged face of his.

"Man, I can see it," he finally mutters, eyes flicking between me and Molly. "You're not bullshitting."

"Never about this," I affirm, my gaze locked on his. The ring in my hand feels like it's pulsating, like Molly's heart and mine are pounding in sync, calling out to him.

"Jake..." Molly's voice is softer now, a murmur that somehow slices through the tension.

His eyes hold mine a beat longer, searching,

digging for the truth in the depths of my soul. And damn if he doesn't find what he's looking for because something shifts in his posture, a loosening of his shoulders, an unclenching of fists that have never swung at me out of anger.

"Fuck," he breathes out, a chuckle without humor. "You really love her, don't you?"

"More than anything," I reply, the words thick with promise.

It's as if a dam breaks inside Jake, and the floodwaters of his rage recede, leaving behind the bedrock of our years of friendship. He looks from me to his sister, the conflict in his expression ebbing away, replaced by something akin to resignation—a surrender to the inevitable.

"Alright." His voice carries the weight of a thousand unsaid things. "Alright, Tanner."

"Jake?" Molly questions, her voice a mix of hope and uncertainty.

"Damn it, Mol, if I say no, will you listen?" He runs a hand down his face, worn from the battle raging inside him seconds ago.

"Probably not," she admits with a sheepish grin.

"Then what choice do I have?" He sighs but there's warmth creeping into those words. "You've got my blessing. But Tanner, so help me God, if you hurt her..."

"I know the drill," I cut in, grinning despite the gravity of the moment.

"Good." Jake nods, then does something that seals the deal more than any words could—he steps forward and pulls us both into a bear hug that says 'family' in a way signatures on a marriage certificate never could.

"Love you, bro," I manage, my voice muffled against his shoulder.

"Love you too, asshole," he grumbles back, but there's a smile in his voice, a reluctant joy that makes my chest tight.

"Thank you, Jake," Molly whispers, her arms wrapped around us both.

As we step back, I catch the shimmer of tears in her eyes, but they're the good kind—the kind that come when you realize your heart's desires are not just dreams anymore. Jake claps my shoulder, a silent promise that he means every word.

"Uh, there's just one problem," I point on.

Molly and Jake both look at me with question marks in their eyes.

She still hasn't said 'yes' yet. I frown at Molly, and she laughs.

Jake chuckles."Go on, then. Ask her properly. I won't get in the way this time."

I turn to Molly, who's watching me with a look that could stop time.

I drop to one knee again, heart hammering in wild rhythm. "Molly, will you—"

"Yes," she breathes out before I can finish, dropping to her knees to meet me, her lips crashing onto mine like waves upon the shore.

"Jesus, get a room," Jake groans, but I barely hear him over the roaring in my ears, the thunderous applause of my heart as I hold the woman I'm going to marry.

"Already did," I mumble against Molly's mouth, laughter bubbling up between kisses.

"Smartass," Jake mutters, but I can tell by the shake of his head and the sliver of a smile that he's already halfway to accepting this new reality.

"Always," I shoot back, winking at him over Molly's shoulder as she pulls me closer.

"Welcome to the family, Tanner," comes his final benediction.

I look down at Molly and realize that's all I'll ever want. A family with her.

EPILOGUE

Five Years Later

Molly

I TWIST THE SOFT, pale yellow ribbon around my fingers as I craft a hairbow. I'm perched on our cushy beige couch that's hugged by bookshelves on either side, stuffed with novels and knick-knacks that tell the story of us. The overhead light casts a warm glow across the room, bouncing off the framed photos of beach trips and lazy Sundays. This house is our love letter, every corner filled with Tanner's strong presence and my softer touch. It's intimate, lived-in—ours.

"Peekaboo!" Tanner's deep laugh rumbles from

behind the armchair where he's hiding, his muscular arms ready to scoop up our little girl when she toddles over.

"Again, Daddy!" Our daughter's voice is a blend of my melody and his timbre. Her tiny feet patter against the hardwood floor as she rounds the chair with a giggle that's pure sunshine. She inherited my wild brunette curls, but those deep blue eyes are all Tanner —wide with delight, reflecting the innocence I so desperately want to protect.

"Gotcha!" Tanner swoops her into the air, and she squeals, her chubby hands reaching for his face. His intensity melts away in these moments, replaced by a tenderness that squeezes my heart every time.

"Mommy, look!" She wriggles in Tanner's secure hold, stretching her arms out to me. "Fly like a birdie!"

"Wow, you're soaring so high!" I put down my crochet project, applauding as if she's just performed the greatest feat. "Like a superhero, huh?"

"Super Lily!" she declares, and Tanner spins her gently before bringing her back down to earth, his biceps flexing instinctively to cushion her landing.

"Best damn hero in town," Tanner agrees, planting a kiss on her forehead. His gaze flicks to me, the silent promise in his eyes still sending that familiar thrill down my spine.

"Mommy, play too!" Lily tugs at my hand, and I let

myself be pulled into their orbit, the three of us a whirlwind of laughter and pretend capes made from dish towels.

"Alright, Super Lily and Captain Daddy," I say, striking a heroic pose that earns another round of giggles. "Let's save the day together."

It's easy, this life with them—a constant dance of love and laughter, and yeah, a fair share of dirty diapers and two a.m. wake-up calls. But I wouldn't trade it for anything. Not when I have Tanner, who can go from fierce warrior to doting father in a heartbeat, and Lily, our perfect little creation who's got his strength and my spirit.

"Come on, heroes," I grin, feeling the heat rise in my cheeks, "let's build a pillow fort!"

And just like that, we're off—diving into cushions, draping blankets, building a fortress fit for the fiercest of families. It's crazy, chaotic, and absolutely perfect.

"Uncle Jake!" Lily's squeal cuts through the fortress tranquility, and her little body wriggles out from under an avalanche of pillows to sprint towards the door. I peek out from our makeshift citadel just in time to see her launch into Jake's open arms, her tiny fingers tangling into his short brown hair.

"Hey, squirt!" Jake chuckles, hoisting her up high before spinning her around, her laughter tinkling like wind chimes in a summer breeze. He's got that easy grin plastered on his face, the one that makes him everyone's instant pal—especially a four-year-old's with energy for days.

"Did I hear something about a pillow fort of justice?" Jake winks at me as he maneuvers into the living room, pretending to stagger under Lily's weight like she's the heaviest thing on earth.

"Indestructible walls," Tanner adds, popping up behind me, his eyes twinkling with silent mirth. "Took some serious Navy SEAL skills."

"Wow, must be some fort," Jake teases, ducking under a blanket draped haphazardly across two chairs. "I'm impressed."

"Uncle Jake builds better forts," Lily declares with a child's brutal honesty, and we all laugh because it's probably true. Jake's always been the king of playtime, ever since we were kids ourselves.

"Alright, alright," Jake says, setting Lily down inside our fortress. "How about I build you a super-duper fort next time, huh?"

"Promise?" Lily holds up her pinky, and Jake links his own with hers in a solemn vow.

"Promise. But hey, I heard it's someone's special day today," Jake says, eyebrow quirked as he looks over at Tanner and me. "Five years, right?"

"Yep, five years of putting up with this guy," I say, nudging Tanner with a teasing smile.

"Putting up? I'm a delight," Tanner protests, wrapping an arm around my waist and pulling me close. His playful facade can't hide the warmth in his eyes though, a warmth that's mirrored in my own heartbeat.

"Which is exactly why I'm here," Jake says, his tone shifting to something more sincere. "I was thinking, you two should have the night off. Go out, celebrate. I'll babysit this little terror."

"Really?" I exchange a look with Tanner, the idea unfurling like a gift. Alone time has been scarce since Lily came bouncing into our world.

"Absolutely. You guys deserve it," Jake insists, ruffling Lily's hair. "And I could use some quality time with my favorite niece."

"Favorite? She's your only niece," Tanner points out with a mock scowl.

"Semantics," Jake shrugs. "So what do you say? Do I get to spoil her rotten tonight or what?"

"Jake, that would be amazing," I breathe out, feeling a swell of gratitude for my brother who's always had our backs.

"Go on then, make those reservations. Paint the town red. Or whatever color you two lovebirds want." Jake grins, already pulling out toys to distract Lily with.

"Thank you," I whisper, squeezing his hand, overwhelmed by his thoughtfulness. Tanner claps him on the back, the two sharing a moment of wordless under-standing. It's moments like these when I know, without a shadow of a doubt, we're not just a family—we're a team, unbreakable.

"Okay, let's leave Uncle Jake to his babysitting duties," Tanner says, his voice low and promising as he guides me away from our cozy chaos, a twinkle of anticipation lighting up his deep blue eyes.

"Bye, Mommy! Bye, Daddy!" Lily calls, already engrossed in a game of space explorer with Jake, her giggles fading as we step out of the house and into what feels like the first breath of freedom in ages.

The door clicks shut behind us, and I lean back into Tanner's solid chest, a playful sigh escaping my lips. "Looks like we have the night all to ourselves," I murmur, pressing my hand over Tanner's as it snakes around my waist.

"Looks that way," Tanner rumbles, his breath warm on my neck. "Do you know what I'm going to do to you tonight, wife?" His fingers trail a tantalizing path just above the hem of my jeans, sending shivers down my spine.

"Not until you at least wine and dine me," I tease.

"Then you better hurry up and get dressed. I don't know how long I can hold off," he warns me.

I scamper upstairs, my heart pounding with excitement. Our bedroom smells like vanilla and musk, a scent as comforting as it is arousing. There's something about getting ready with Tanner nearby, our anticipation tangling together like the sheets we'll later unravel.

"Hey, sailor," I tease, watching him peel off his day clothes, revealing that body sculpted from duty and strength. "Planning to wear anything special tonight?"

"Only if you count the cologne you love," he shoots back with a wink, dabbing a bit on his jawline—the spot I'll surely be kissing later.

"Keep that up, and we might never leave this room," I laugh, slipping out of my own casual wear. I choose a dress that hugs every curve—a deep red, the color of passion, of ripe cherries, of the flush I feel creeping up my cheeks.

"Molly," Tanner's voice is a low growl as he takes me in. "You're trying to kill me, aren't you?"

"Wouldn't dream of it," I retort, fastening the clasp on my necklace with hands that tremble ever so slightly. "Not when I've got plans for you."

Tanner slips into a crisp shirt, the muscles of his back shifting enticingly beneath the fabric. I'm drawn to him, my fingertips grazing along his belt, feeling the thrum of his pulse through the denim.

"Plans, huh?" He turns, trapping my hand against him, his eyes darkening. "I like the sound of that."

"Patience, Mr. Navy SEAL," I whisper, freeing my hand with a smirk. "We've got all night."

"Then let's not waste another minute." Tanner offers his arm, gentlemanly, but the promise in his touch is anything but polite.

As we head downstairs, I catch our reflection in the hallway mirror—Tanner, handsome and fierce; me, flushed with desire. We're a picture of eager yearning, poised on the edge of a night filled with laughter, whispers, and the kind of fiery connection that burns hotter each year.

"Gotcha!" Jake's voice echoes playfully through the living room as he sweeps our daughter up into his arms, spinning her around until her laughter becomes a melodious backdrop to the evening. Her little hands grasp at his stubbled cheek, a gesture so tender it squeezes my heart.

"Fly, Uncle Jake, fly!" she squeals, and Jake complies with another twirl, pretending to be an airplane. She's the spitting image of Tanner, all daring and bright-eyed wonder, but when she giggles, it's my own joy reflected in her sound.

"Look at you, my brave little pilot," he coos, setting

her down gently but keeping one hand secured around her waist. She wobbles on her feet, still dizzy from the flight, her curls a wild halo around her flushed face.

"Again!" she demands, always hungry for more adventure, and I can't help but admire her spirit.

"Give me two secs, kiddo," Jake says, glancing over his shoulder with a grin. "Gotta make sure these two lovebirds get out the door first."

I slip my arm through Tanner's, feeling the coiled strength beneath his suit jacket. He looks every bit the dashing rogue tonight, his blue eyes alight with mischief and promise.

"Remember, bed by eight and no sugar after seven," I remind Jake, though I know it's like preaching to the choir. He knows the drill better than anyone.

"Roger that, sis," he salutes with a wink. "Now go, enjoy your night of unfettered passion and debauchery."

"Unfettered passion" is definitely on the menu, and I can feel its heat simmering just below my skin, waiting for release.

"Behave," I tease him, leaning in to plant a kiss on our daughter's forehead. "Mommy and Daddy will be back before you even miss us."

But she's not even studying us. She only has eyes for her favorite playmate—Uncle Jake.

"Alright, let's give these lovebirds some space." Jake

scoops her into his arms again, tickling her sides and eliciting a peal of laughter that fills the room with light.

"Have fun, Jake," Tanner rumbles, his voice low and intimate as he nods his thanks.

"Always do," Jake replies, already pulling out a board game from the shelf. "Go on, get out of here!"

Tanner pulls me close, his hand warm against the small of my back, guiding me to the door. We step out into the night, and the chill in the air is a delicious contrast to the warmth we leave behind.

"Freedom," I sigh, feeling the anticipation fizzing through my veins as we head towards the car. The moon hangs low, a witness to our escape, while the stars twinkle with knowing approval.

"Ready to make some memories?" Tanner asks, his voice a velvet promise that wraps around me, enticing as the night itself.

"Let's make the kind that keeps us up till dawn," I answer, my pulse racing as I imagine the hours ahead —undressing each other with eager hands, exploring familiar paths with new fervor, whispering secrets between kisses that taste of forever.

As Tanner opens the cab door for me, I slide in, the fabric of my dress whispering against my thighs, a prelude to the symphony of sensation I know awaits.

The cab door shuts with a soft thud behind us, sealing us in our private cocoon of leather and longing.

Tanner's fingers find mine, setting the night ablaze with possibilities. I watch his profile, rugged and assured, the streetlights casting shadows that play over his chiseled jaw. He catches me staring and winks, the blue of his eyes sparking mischief.

"Ever been to La Petite Fleur?" he teases.

"Only in my dreams," I quip, feeling the corners of my lips rise. "Do they serve fantasies on a plate there?"

"Only the ones you can taste, touch, and savor," he says, his voice a low rumble that sends shivers dancing down my spine.

La Petite Fleur is an intimate haven, nestled between towering buildings like a secret whispered between lovers. The maître d' knows Tanner by name, and his smile widens when he sees us together. "Mr. and Mrs. James, right this way." His accent is a caress that beckons us deeper into the restaurant's embrace.

Candlelight flickers on linen-clad tables, each a small island adrift in a sea of soft music and murmured conversations. Our table is a secluded alcove, petals strewn across the surface like kisses waiting to be claimed. Tanner pulls out my chair, and I sink into it, the scent of roses wrapping around us, a fragrant reminder of our first official date after we told Jake about us.

"Happy anniversary, wife," he says, his hand

finding mine across the table, skin against skin like a promise renewed.

"Happy anniversary, husband" I echo, squeezing his hand, my heart thrumming a rhythm that mirrors the candle's dance.

Wine arrives, crimson and bold, mirroring the flush of excitement on my cheeks. We toast to us, to now, to the moments that weave the tapestry of our shared life. Tanner's gaze holds mine, intense and unwavering, and I lose myself in the depths of his oceanic eyes.

"Remember that time we got lost hiking?" he chuckles, breaking the spell with a memory that has us both laughing.

"Lost? You mean that 'scenic detour' you took us on?" I tease, recalling the hours spent wandering, the eventual relief of finding our path, the adventure tinged with the thrill of the unknown. The way Tanner fucked me in the tent…

"Best detour of my life," he grins, the heat in his expression not solely attributed to the wine. "It led me right where I needed to be."

Our meal unfolds like a seduction—each course more enticing than the last. We feed each other tastes of decadence, forks flirting, our eyes saying more than words ever could.

"Every moment with you is a reason to celebrate," Tanner murmurs, tracing the back of my hand with his thumb, igniting tiny wildfires with every sweep. "You're all I've ever wanted, Molly. I'm the luckiest man alive to have you."

Laughter spills from us, easy and genuine, mixing with the clinking of cutlery and soft jazz that caresses the air. I revel in the joy of us, the perfect synchrony that comes from years of loving and growing together.

Our dinner lingers, a slow burn that builds to a crescendo, and when we finally stand to leave, Tanner's arm slips around my waist, drawing me close as we step back out into the cool night.

Tanner's hand finds mine in the back of the cab, his fingers a silent promise of what's to come. His touch is both familiar and electric, a current that never fails to set my skin ablaze. I squeeze back, my pulse quickening with each block we put between us and the restaurant.

"Can't wait to get you alone," he whispers, lips brushing my earlobe, sending shivers down my spine. The playful glint in his deep blue eyes tells me he's as ready as I am to abandon all pretense of patience.

"Who says we have to wait?" I tease, inching closer, letting my knee brush against his in a suggestive dance.

"Here I was thinking you liked the anticipation," Tanner counters, but he pulls me into him, his strong arms coiling around my waist like steel bands.

"Only when it leads to satisfaction," I quip, a smirk playing on my lips. My breath hitches as his hands trail lower, boldly claiming territory over the fabric of my dress, stoking the fires within me.

"Then let's make sure you're thoroughly satisfied," he growls, and the raw edge in his voice is all it takes—my body ignites with need, desire pooling at the very thought of his touch.

The cab pulls over, and we spill out onto the sidewalk, barely managing to keep our hands off each other long enough for the driver to speed away. Once inside our home, Tanner kicks the door shut with his foot, and his mouth crashes onto mine, hot and demanding.

Thank god Jake has already taken Lily home with him.

I'm lost in the taste of my husband, the feel of his rough hands roaming over my body with an urgency that matches the pounding of my heart. Clothes become inconsequential, discarded carelessly as we navigate toward the bedroom. Every caress from Tanner is searing, every kiss laced with hunger.

We fall onto the mattress, our bodies entwined on the bed we've shared so many nights before, yet tonight there's a carnal intensity that feels almost sacred. He's slow and deliberate as he worships every inch of my body, his lips tracing paths that leave me gasping, begging for more. I arch into him, craving the fullness only he can provide.

"God, Molly, you're so damn beautiful," Tanner breathes out, his gaze locked onto mine as he positions himself at my entrance. With one powerful thrust, he fills me completely, eliciting a moan that echoes in the quiet of our room.

"More, please," I plead, nails digging into the muscles of his back, urging him deeper. Each movement is a testament to our unending lust—a rhythm that drives us higher, teetering on the brink of ecstasy.

"Oh, I'm going to give you everything, baby," Tanner vows, his pace relentless, each stroke sending me higher and higher until my eyes are rolling back in my head.

The world narrows to just us, to the heat and the love and the sheer force of our connection.

And then I feel Tanner come inside me, and it triggers my own orgasm.

In the aftermath, Tanner's chest heaves against mine, his heartbeat thunderous against my skin. I trace the outline of Tanner's tattoos with a fingertip, our sweat-slicked bodies still joined in the most intimate of embraces. His breath dances along my neck.

"Happy anniversary, my love," he murmurs, sealing the vow with a kiss that's tender yet still thrumming with the aftershocks of our passion.

"Mmm-hmm," I mumble.

"God, I love you," he chuckles, the rumble of his voice vibrating through me. He shifts slightly, and pleasure flickers, reminding me that the fire between us is never fully extinguished.

"Love you more," I tease, tilting my head to catch his lips in a lazy kiss. It's soft, a mere brush really, but it's enough to make my heart expand so fiercely I fear it might burst.

I yawn, completely sated. "Will it always be like this between us, Tanner?"

He strokes my head tenderly, and I arch up into his touch, practically purring with satisfaction. "Always," he affirms, and it's the last thing I hear before drifting off, safe in the arms of my Navy SEAL, my love, my everything.

Want a free book from Emma Bray? Go to www. authoremmabray.com.